ASHPET

An Appalachian Tale

retold by Joanne Compton

illustrated by Kenn Compton

Holiday House/New York

For our sisters—Judy, Eleanor, and Kathy,
and for the generations of sisters who have come before us:
Mae, Jo, and Isabelle;
Josephine, Emma, Louise, and Minnie;
Annie and Lelia;
Della, Myrtle, and Ethel

Text copyright © 1994 by Joanne Ward Compton
Illustrations copyright © 1994 by Kenn Compton
ALL RIGHTS RESERVED
Printed in the United States of America
FIRST EDITION

Library of Congress Cataloging-in-Publication Data
Compton, Joanne.
Ashpet : an Appalachian tale / retold by Joanne Compton ;
illustrated by Kenn Compton. — 1st ed.
p.   cm.
Summary: In this Appalachian variant of the Cinderella tale,
old Granny helps Ashpet attend the church picnic where she charms
Doc Ellison's son but loses one of her fancy red shoes.
ISBN 0-8234-1106-0
[1. Fairy tales. 2. Folklore—United States.] I. Compton, Kenn,
ill. II. Title.
PZ8.C755As   1994   93-16034   CIP   AC
398.21—dc20
[E]

AUTHOR'S NOTE

The story of Cinderella is very old. The earliest recorded version is "Yeh-shien," found in a Chinese book dating from 850 A.D. Since then, hundreds of Cinderella variants have been collected from around the world. In each version, the details of the story are influenced by the setting and culture of the storytellers.

The Grimm Brothers, in their first collection of folktales, *Children's and Household Tales* (1812), told the German story of "Aschenputtel." European settlers probably brought a similar version to the Southern Appalachian area of America and eventually told it as "Ashpet."

Richard Chase recorded the Ashpet story and published it in his collection, *Grandfather Tales* (Houghton Mifflin, 1948). In the Appalachian version, Ashpet is not an orphaned daughter but a servant girl, "bound out" to a widow and her two daughters. In our retelling, I have recast the king's son as a more likely mountain character—the doctor's son. We hope that children will enjoy reading this American story of Cinderella and will compare it to the other versions they may have heard.

—*Joanne Compton*

Long ago, in a cabin deep in the shadow of Eagle's Nest Mountain, lived a serving girl called Ashpet. She'd been hired out since she was a young girl to the Widow Hooper and her two daughters, Myrtle and Ethel.

All day long, the Hooper women thought of chores for Ashpet to do. "After you're done washin' up, there's firewood that wants bustin', and our supper to cook. And don't forget to tend to the animals."

Now Ethel and Myrtle were as ugly as they were lazy, but Ashpet was fresh-faced and regular-featured. Those two girls were so jealous that whenever anyone came to their cabin, they stuck Ashpet under a wash-tub. And they never let her go anywhere.

In the hot months of summer, when the crops were laid by, the folk of Eagle's Nest Mountain gathered for a big church meeting. Every year the Widow Hooper, Myrtle, and Ethel got out their finest clothes, packed a picnic hamper, and set off. And every year, they left Ashpet behind to do her chores.

It happened that one year, on the evening before the meeting, Ashpet stayed up all night washing, ironing, and mending the girls' dresses. She was so busy, she didn't notice that the fire had gone out in the fireplace.

Widow Hooper was furious the next morning and called to Myrtle.

"Run over the ridge to old Granny's house and borry us some fire."

"Granny's too peculiar," snapped Myrtle. "Anyway, that's Ashpet's job. Make her go!"

"Ashpet can't. She's gotta finish these dresses, and if we don't have fire, we can't heat water, and if we can't heat water, we can't get our bath. Now scoot!"

Myrtle sure didn't want to go, but she knew when her mama meant business. So she ran over the ridge to Granny's place and stood out in the yard hollering, "I come fer fire, old woman!"

No answer. Myrtle inched a little closer to the cabin. Finally she heard a small scratchy voice say, "First you come in and brush my hair."

Myrtle wasn't about to go inside. So she hollered back, "I ain't coming in there with you, old woman. Jes' you fetch me out some fire."

Well, Granny wouldn't give fire to anyone acting so uppity, so Myrtle went home empty-handed.

Widow Hooper was fit to be tied. "Ethel," she commanded, "you run to Granny's and see if you can do better than this worthless sister of yours."

So Ethel headed over the ridge, and the same thing happened again. When Ethel refused to comb Granny's hair, Granny didn't give her any fire. She, too, went home empty-handed, and her mama was mad as a wet hen.

Widow Hooper jerked Ashpet up by the elbow and shoved her out the door. "You get yerself over to Granny's and don't come back until you got the fire."

Ashpet skedaddled over the ridge and went up and knocked on the front door of the cabin. She didn't hear anything, so she called out, "My name is Ashpet, and I've come to borry some fire, please."

"You may. But first won't you brush my hair out for me? My brush is jes' on the table here."

Ashpet went inside, picked up the brush, and began to pull it through the old lady's hair.

Granny asked, "Are you goin' to the big church meetin' with the rest of them Hooper women?"

"Don't reckon I will! I'm just a serving girl!" snorted Ashpet. "I got me all these chores to do. Don't have time to go down to the meetin'."

"Well, mebbe I'll be by your cabin later on," answered Granny.

When Granny's hair was all combed, Ashpet asked, "May I have some fire now?"

Granny crooked her mouth in a toothless grin. "Of course, child, help yerself."

Once home, Ashpet built up the fire and heated pot after pot of water. The sisters and their mama bathed, and Ashpet helped them into their dresses.

"We're going now! Ashpet, you best git this cabin cleaned up 'fore we git back or there'll be more trouble than you can think about. Let's go, girls!" announced Widow Hooper.

No sooner were they gone than there was a tapping noise on the path outside the cabin. Ashpet looked out the window and saw Granny making her way up the steps to the porch.

Ashpet went outside to meet her. But Granny walked right past, poked her head in the door, muttered something under her breath, and tapped her walking stick three times on the floor. The door slammed shut, Granny came out, and the cabin began to shake. Ashpet could hear furniture scraping, dishes rattling, and cupboard doors banging. It sounded like the whole place was about to come apart.

"What's goin' on in there, Granny?" asked Ashpet.
"Don't you worry 'bout it, child."

Just then the door flew open. Ashpet peered inside. The cabin was straighter than Ashpet believed could be possible. The dishes were washed, dried, and put away. The clothes were clean and folded, and the beds were made. Even the floor was swept. And by the fireplace was the prettiest red calico dress that Ashpet had ever seen and a pair of new red shoes.

"Don't you jes' stand there, child," said Granny. "Change your clothes and git along to the meetin'! Jes' remember this one thing: come back home this evenin' before midnight."

And with that the old woman was gone.

Quick as a wink Ashpet cleaned up, then tried on the new dress and shoes. She admired herself in the dingy, old-looking glass hanging on the wall. Never had she looked so pretty. Then she danced across the cabin, out into the sunshine, and down the road to the meeting.

By the time Ashpet got to the church, the preacher had been going on all morning. Ashpet slipped quietly into a seat near the back, but she looked so pretty, folks started whispering. With all the commotion going on, even the doctor's son swiveled his head around to look.

"A-HEM!" The preacher cleared his throat, then set-
tled back into his sermon. Finally, late in the afternoon,
he ran out of something to say, and the crowd sang a
hymn and broke up for supper on the lawn.

Widow Hooper, Myrtle, and Ethel stopped the doctor's son and asked him to share their picnic basket.
But his eyes were only on Ashpet. He took the basket
from Widow Hooper, thanked her very kindly for it, and
made his way to where Ashpet was standing.

The Hoopers flew into a temper. "Why, the very nerve of that girl!" exclaimed Ethel.

"Who does she think she is?" sniffed Myrtle.

"We don't have to stand for that!" Widow Hooper declared. "We're going home." They turned heel and headed back up the road to their cabin.

Ashpet and the doctor's son found a quiet spot by the river to enjoy the supper. Time slipped on by as they walked and talked and laughed long into the night. Just as they were strolling past Benford's footbridge, Ashpet remembered what Granny had said about being home before midnight. How could she get away? Quickly, she kicked one of her shoes off into the bushes.

"I declare! It's time for me to get on home!" Ashpet cried.

"Let me walk you there," said the doctor's son.

"All right," Ashpet answered. "But first, how 'bout findin' my shoe? I believe I lost it back somewhere on the road."

As soon as the doctor's son turned back, Ashpet took off through the woods.

When she got to the cabin, she hid her dress and put her rags back on. But she didn't take off her fancy shoe. That night, she fell asleep smiling.

The next morning, Widow Hooper and Ethel woke Ashpet by poking her with their bony fingers.

"Wake up, lazybones!" sneered Ethel. "Tell us where you were when we got home last night!"

"Who do you think you are, disappearin' at night and layin' in bed in the morning?" fussed Widow Hooper.

Ashpet looked down. "It won't happen again," she answered.

"You can be sure it won't, you good-fer-nothin' slug-abed! Now git out of bed and fix us some breakfast!" ordered Widow Hooper.

Just as Ashpet got to work, terrible shrieks came from the loft.

"Mama! Mama! Mama!"

"Myrtle, what's got into you, child?" asked the Widow Hooper.

"He's coming! He's coming!" Myrtle screamed.

"Get ahold of yourself, girl, and tell me who's coming!"

Myrtle's voice was quivering. "It's Doc Ellison's boy! I can see him out the window. He's coming down the road right towards our house!"

By that time Ethel had run to the front of the cabin and flung open the door. "I can see him too, Mama! He's coming this way all right!"

Widow Hooper cried, "Quick, Ethel, shut the door and git back in the loft with Myrtle! Both of you, gussy yourselves up some. I wonder why on earth he's coming to visit us?"

Ashpet quickly offered, "I'll fix up something for him to eat."

"You'll do no such thing," snapped the Widow. "It wouldn't be right for somebody as dirty as you to be seen by somebody as good as Doc Ellison's boy. You get under this washtub and stay until I let you out."

Widow Hooper had just shoved Ashpet under the tub when she heard a knock at the door.

"Won't you please come in, sir?" asked Widow Hooper.

"Thanky, Ma'am," answered Doc Ellison's son. "I don't aim to take much of your time. You see, I've been goin' to every cabin up and down Eagle's Nest Mountain. I'm lookin' for the girl who lost this shoe at the meetin' last night. Could it belong to someone in this house?"

"I'm sure it belongs to one of my charmin' daughters," purred Widow Hooper. "Oh, Ethel dear, please come down and try this here shoe on fer the doctor's boy."

Ethel came down from the loft and sat down on the washtub. She pushed and shoved and twisted her foot this way and that, but the shoe just wouldn't fit.

"Don't look like it's goin' to fit, Ma'am," said the doctor's son. "I'll not trouble you anymore."

"Wait! I have another daughter! It must be her shoe!" exclaimed Widow Hooper. "Myrtle, honey, please come and try this shoe on for Doc Ellison's boy."

Lickety-split Myrtle scurried down the ladder, snatched the shoe, and crammed her foot into it. Her foot wasn't as wide as Ethel's, but it was a lot longer. Even though her toes fit just fine, her heel would not go in.

The doctor's son slid off the shoe and shook his head. "I'll just be going now, Ma'am." He tipped his hat and opened the door to leave. As he did, a big black bird flew past him, grabbed the shoe in its beak, and swooped around the room. The doctor's son chased the bird, shouting, "Gimme that back, you ole crow!" But the bird stayed just ahead of the boy.

Round and round it went, until finally, it dropped the shoe by the overturned washtub. As the doctor's son leaped for the shoe, he landed on the tub and knocked it right side up. There sat Ashpet, wearing the other shoe.

The doctor's son gaped at Ashpet in her rags. "Are you the one?"

"That shoe sure looks like the mate to this one," said Ashpet, holding out her foot. "Try it and see."

The boy knelt down and slipped the shoe on Ashpet. It fit perfectly.

"Ma'am," he said to Ashpet, "would you consent to marry me?"

"I believe I'd like that," she replied.

Myrtle and Ethel began to cry. Widow Hooper shook her head in anger. "You can't marry her! She's hired out to me for two more years!"

"I reckon this'll pay you for your trouble," the doctor's son said, and tossed the Widow Hooper a purse.

Without looking back, Ashpet walked out the door to marry the doctor's son.

It didn't take long for the whole story to spread around Eagle's Nest Mountain. Folks poked so much fun at the Hooper women for how they'd treated Ashpet that the Widow and her girls were shamed into moving clear over to Crabtree Cove.

As for Ashpet and the doctor's son, from then on, they were as happy as could be.